Toby the Trilby

and the
Forgotten City

Angela Castillo

To Wes. You are so loved

CONTENTS

Thank you to my husband and children for putting up with your writing wife and momma.

1

FLIGHT DREAMS

Every object in the city made its own sound. Buildings shifted and groaned on shaky foundations never designed to stand so long without repair. Ancient wooden poles stood in rows throughout the city. When the wind changed, they squeaked, and rusted wires grated against their sides.

The creak of the fence was different. It beckoned to Emory, invited him to press in, to pursue adventure. The tight wires held a secret he scarcely dared to fathom: a possible escape.

He pulled the twisted metal apart to create a hole for his small body to squeeze through. Rivers of dirt and sweat streaked down his face but couldn't cover his grin. Today might be the day his dream came true.

Emory pushed through thorns and brush. *Wish I could just make a path.* He pulled a twig out of his thick brown hair. A beaten trail might catch someone's attention. If he was followed, everything would be over.

He reached the warehouse, and his hand brushed against the side. "Ouch!" Though the sun drifted below the tree line, the metal was still hot.

The boy skirted the building until he reached a sliding door. Using all his body weight, he forced the panel sideways.

A padlock hung from the hasp in two jagged pieces. For forty years the warehouse had been left untouched. Emory spent days filing down the lock in the hope he'd find a treasure inside. He had not been disappointed.

Slats of light rested on hundreds of dumpster-sized objects, covered by layers of dust. Earth moving vehicles, known as 'tanks,' were still lined up and ready to fight in the ancient wars. Emory couldn't imagine a world with enough humans to drive them all at once.

Now the hulking beasts slept, useless and frail. Even if they could be powered up again, they could never push through the dense forest surrounding the city. Animals and desperate people lurked in the darkened woods, waiting for easy prey.

Emory turned a crank and gear teeth caught on a chain. A giant panel in the roof yawned open to usher in precious light. Only half an hour remained before darkness fell. Maybe enough time. He was so close.

Dust motes patterned the light. Rays fell on the machine and highlighted the areas he had been able to reach and polish. Even after months spent with her gigantic form, her beauty still took his breath away.

She towered over his head. Her thick metal blades, though covered in dust and cobwebs, begged for motion.

Emory smiled at his reflection in the smooth, black side of the machine. The storage area only held a single flying craft, and this was probably the last type created before the disaster. Any other vessel would have depended on fuel impossible to find, but not this model.

Emory tugged a thick manual out of his pack. "TEK-CONDOR." He traced the faded block letters. Creases and smudges filled each page. Night after night, he had poured over every word. He'd searched dozens of rooms in the warehouse to find the equipment and parts detailed on each page.

A storage container leaned against one wall. Emory rummaged under a pile of rags on the shelf and pulled out a cylindrical object, about the size of two fists clenched together. His hands shook with excitement while he examined the metal surface. No cracks or holes. The boy cradled the capsule, heavy for its size, and climbed into the helicopter. He pulled down a lever, placed the fuel pod in a tank, and clicked it shut.

So far, so good. This was really happening! He picked up his manual again. Only one chapter troubled him: "Instructions for the Co-Pilot." Sonda didn't even know about the helicopter yet and probably never heard of such a machine. Could she help him fly? Would she be scared?

No, Sonda wouldn't be afraid. The wind would blow her dark curls like wild clouds around her head, and she'd smile for the first time since-- he didn't know how long ago. Since probably before their mother had died.

But what if something went wrong? What if they crashed to the ground in a blackened mess and he never got to find out what happened next? He pursed his lips in a determined line. Everything would be fine.

Emory slid into the pilot's seat and ran through the list of operations like he had a hundred times--during chores, through evening prayers, and in the darkness of his room while grasping for sleep.

Check the instrument panel
Flip the fuel line lever
Push the engine control forward

Dashboard lights glowed. His mouth hung open while dials on the pressure gauges swayed. The machine trembled and the giant rotary blades turned. A roar filled the inside of the helicopter, his ears, his mind, his entire being.

In his excitement, Emory almost forgot himself and let the machine lift through the opening in the roof and into the sky.

Can't risk a test flight, someone might see me. He pulled the levers back up again, and the blades slowed, then stopped. The lights winked off, one by one.

Emory hopped to the ground on trembling legs and looked up at the mighty machine. She seemed to be holding her breath, just waiting for him to reveal their destination.

"Don't worry, I'm just gonna get my sister." He patted the sleek side. "I'll be back tomorrow."

###

Barn owls gave chilling cries from overhead. White forms swooped down into the field before Toby. A startled squeak announced the end of a small creature and the beginning of an evening meal.

Tears trickled down Toby's cheeks and he sniffed and rubbed his nose. When he closed his eyes he could still see her. Pale skin, white hair that normally puffed around her face like cotton tufts, but today had been curled and arranged by Gramble Lenora's careful hands. Her features, severe and firm in life, softened by eternal peace. Gramble Colleen had gone to be with Father.

Two months before, they all noticed little changes. Gramble Colleen's quick step turned into a shuffle. She spent fewer hours with her beloved microscopes and test tubes and more time reading the Bible, Father's book. For she had come to God at last, and had been baptized by Gramble Edward in the same little underground stream where Toby had first heard Father's voice.

Gramble Colleen preferred the underground fortress for most of her life, but in the last days she came to stay in the little house on the surface. She spent many hours on the front porch, letting the breeze cool her wrinkled skin. One morning Gramble Shana found her, gone ahead to adventures Toby could only dream about.

Death was not new to Toby, but he'd never experienced the loss of someone so close to him, with a life so entwined with his own. Gramble Colleen had been the one to help Gramble Gregory splice human and cat DNA together, place the tiny embryo in a glass womb, and tend to his growth.

The grambles had called him a 'Trilby,' the only one of his kind in the world. For fifteen years they had cared for him and taught him everything they knew.

A soft object tickled Toby's chin and he looked down. He had grabbed his tail, a habit from childhood only returned to in moments of extreme emotion. Tears soaked the thick, brown fur.

If Gramble Colleen could see him now, she would say "Enough boo-hooing over an old woman. Get back to enjoying your own life!"

Earlier today, during the simple funeral service, a feeling had crept over him.

13

Gramble Edward stood over the grave and read Bible verses. The other grambles listened, along with the Professor and his daughter, Zareena. Tinga, Jurn and Mia, children who had come to live with them over the last three years, huddled together, faces shining with tears.

Now, in the velvet evening, the thoughts pushed into his mind again. *Is Heaven a true place? Is God real?* Doubts Toby hadn't considered for years had bubbled to his mind's surface. He wanted to yank out these ideas and throw their writhing forms into the dirt, but they stuck. If only he could be sure--perhaps the pain in his heart wouldn't throb so much.

A noise in the bush pulled Toby out of his pondering. His large, pointed ears perked and he sniffed the air. Human. And someone who didn't belong to his community. He slowly removed his black gloves. No one had ever approached the caverns without an invitation. The cavern group couldn't afford for outsiders to find the massive storage facilities and supplies they harbored underground. His fingers stretched, and claws emerged from the tips.

A person came from behind him and touched his arm. "Hey, little brother." Mia held a lantern, and her golden hair glinted in its light. Though Mia was actually younger than him by three months, his head barely reached her shoulder.

He raised a finger to his lips. Her eyes widened when she saw his claws.

The bushes rustled again. A girl in ragged clothing stepped forward.

"Hey, Cat Kid."

"Marabella," Toby sighed. "What on Earth are you doing here?"

"Wanted to check on the little 'uns."

When Toby had last seen Marabella, over a year ago, her face had been streaked with blood and dirt from a battle. Now she seemed to be in good health.

"How did you find us?" Toby looked over her shoulder. "Is anyone else with you?" His past dealings with Marabella had not been pleasant.

"Naw. I've been lookin' for your place forever. Just got lucky, I guess. Good thing, too." She held out her hand. A dirty piece of cloth covered one wrist. "Cut myself and thought ya might have stuff to fix me up."

Mia looked over at Toby and raised her pale eyebrows.

Toby nodded slowly. "Of course we can help. And Tinga and Jurn wonder about you every day. They'll be relieved to know you're all right. Come on, the house is over here."

Toby led the way through the thin grove of trees, across the yard and up the steps of the porch. "Welcome to our home." He pushed open the door. "Gramble Lenora, there's someone here for you to meet!"

Light greeted them from a small table, where a candle flickered. The rest of the house seemed wrapped around this glow, with honey-gold wooden walls and cheery homemade quilts covering the furniture.

Gramble Lenora's bulky form filled the end of one sofa. She looked up from her novel, and light glinted on her fiercely dyed, scarlet hair. "A newcomer? Is everything all right, Toby?"

Before he could answer, the back door opened and Gramble Shana came in from the cottage in the back yard where she lived with her husband, Gramble Edward.. She placed a basket of eggs on the counter by the stove. Her long, white braid fell over her shoulder and tangled in the

15

fringe of her knitted shawl. "Toby, I thought I heard you pass by... Who do we have here?"

"This house is so clean." Marabella stared down at her dirty hands. "I'll go outside."

"Nonsense!" Gramble Lenora sprang up, her shapeless dress billowing. "You come right over and wash those hands. There's some beans and corn bread left from supper, though Toby and Jurn did their best, growing boys and all."

The elderly woman lumbered through the room to light more candles on the counters. She grabbed Marabella's shirt sleeve and tugged her over to the sink. "Just need to start the pump, darlin'."

Marabella pulled the bandage from her hand.

Mia came over. "Looks painful. I'll get my medical kit and patch it up for you."

"Who is she?" Gramble Shana murmured to Toby. Lines of concern surrounded her kind blue eyes.

Gramble Lenora turned back from the sink and tilted her head.

"She helped lead Dread's gang." Toby said while Marabella took the bar of soap Gramble Lenora handed her and turned it over in her hands. *Probably never seen soap before.* "She's kinda like Tinga and Jurn's sister, I guess."

"Didn't she have you tied up to a tree once? Is she safe?" Gramble Lenora reached over to a shelf and grabbed a rolling pin.

"I heard that!" Marabella whipped around, spattering the floor with drops of water. Her eyes flashed. "I'm not gonna put those kids in danger by ratting you all out, if that's what you're gettin' at."

Gramble Lenora set down the rolling pin and gave her a regal, tight lipped gaze.

"Ma'am." Marbella looked down.

"Why don't you come have some supper?" Toby set a plate of food on the table.

Mia returned from the other room. She dabbed medicine on Marabella's hand and wrapped it with a clean bandage. "The cut's not too deep. I don't think you'll need stitches but I'll have to change the dressing tomorrow."

"Where are Tinga and Jurn, anyhow?" Marabella plunked down in the chair and grabbed a chunk of corn bread.

"Gramble Shana went to tell them you're here." Toby took a piece of bread from the bowl. "They're feeding the animals."

"Animals? I didn't hear no animals." Crumbs flecked Marabella's lips.

"Not everything is as it seems." Gramble Lenora poured her a glass of milk.

"Fresh milk?" Marabella grabbed the glass so fast some of the white liquid splashed on the table. She gulped it down, then wiped off the resulting moustache with the back of her hand. "That's good stuff. I bet it tastes better than Vibrance, though I ain't ever tried it."

"What's Vibrance?" Although Toby had seen films and read books about every imaginable subject, he had never heard of this drink.

"From the city of the forgotten." Marabella squinted up at him. "I went there a little while after I left you guys, when I was following Leader to find my gang. Anyways, a place in the city sells this stuff called Vibrance. Makes people all loopy."

"Did you find the other kids?" Toby changed the subject. "Is everyone all right?"

"Course I did." She dismissed the question with a wave of her bandaged hand. "Fat and sassy, every one of 'em. Happy to be fed and followin' Leader. They didn't care if he smacked 'em around sometimes. I mean, he's fillin' their tummies better than Dread ever did."

Toby sighed. "Well, at least they're alive."

"Don't know why you'd care so much 'bout us. We did mean stuff to you."

"Tinga and Jurn are family now," Gramble Lenora began to clear the supper dishes. "They do their part around here and we love them. God tells us to have compassion for everyone in this dangerous world. Especially children."

Marabella licked the last few crumbs off her fingers. "I met some people in the city who talked about God like you folks do."

Toby's ears perked up. "Really? How many people? Did they have meetings?"

Marabella bit her lip. "What did they call it? Oh yeah, they called their group a church. They try to help folks, same as you guys. Gave me some food. They wanted me to stay, but, you know."

Toby's heart leapt inside his chest. Sometimes Father spoke to him out loud, but often he felt a simple awareness in his soul, a need to pay attention. "I would love to find a church."

Marabella's eyes narrowed. "I wouldn't go pokin' around that city. Most of the people are sloshed on Vibrance. And Leader was pretty close, though his trucks would never make it to the walls. I'm guessing he don't know about it yet, 'cause he'd of taken everything by now."

18

Tinga and Jurn burst through the door. Their faces glowed with matching freckles. Tinga threw herself at Marabella for a hug while Jurn hung back and smiled.

Marabella touched the smooth pigtails hanging down Tinga's back. "Look at you," she whispered. "They fixed you up, didn't they?"

Maybe she really has changed. Toby scooted out from the table. "We all need to get some rest. You can sleep in Tinga's room, if she doesn't mind."

The little girl nodded, her eyes shining.

"Don't stay up too long." Gramble Lenora kissed Tinga on the cheek. "If I know Toby, he's planning a new adventure. Tomorrow will be a busy day for everyone."

2

ADVENTURING AGAIN

Strains of music, hollow and faint, floated through the door at the Palace of Dreams. In Emory's house, music was created with voices and hands. People sang in service every Sunday. Sometimes during chores, a child would begin a song in a high, sweet voice, and everyone else chimed along.

Olders spoke of years past when sounds were recorded, then played on electronic devices anywhere and at any time. Now few musical instruments remained from the past.

Emory did not know if the Palace musicians had taught themselves to play, or were instructed by olders, but the melody tripped and skipped in a constant stream, day and night. Dancers needed a reason to dance.

The old woman in front of him scratched the door with a gnarled hand. "Please," she rasped. "Please ask my Henry to come to me. I just want to see my boy for a moment. He's the only one I have left. Please, I haven't seen him for three days..."

This started a chain reaction throughout the group of mostly women and children. They wailed and beat on the wall.

Emory was lucky; his sister's trinkets would only buy her a few hours of dancing time. Some people waited much longer to catch a glimpse of a loved one.

He only saw Sonda every now and then when she'd come by the church for a few mouthfuls of food. Wild-eyed and scrambling, his sister usually begged him for memory objects, the Palace's demanded payment. But sometimes her mind would clear a bit, and she'd bring up a plan to journey through the forest and find new treasures for Simper, the keeper of the Palace.

Emory knew what happened to mem-seekers. They disappeared into the woods and never came back.

But what if he could use the idea to get his sister into the helicopter? If they found a new, bright city so far away no one in town had even heard about it, she could live without the Vibrance and be happy for real. Perhaps then she could learn how to dance on her own.

He wanted to burst through the door like an autumn storm, find his sister and tell her about his plan. But he was only eleven, too young to be allowed in the palace, and besides, his last treasures were gone. The locket with the picture of his grandmother, the wooden elephant his father had carved in long winter evenings--all stolen by his sister to be thrown into Simper's hoard.

Emory shuffled from foot to foot. His chin edged closer to the neckline of his rough garment. For a moment he wavered, then sank to the ground and curled into a ball.

His eyes fluttered as a shadow fell over his face. Right before he drifted off, a familiar chuckle sounded in his ear. Strong arms picked him up and carried him away.

Mia placed the last bag in the roamer's storage bin and turned to Toby. "Are you going to need anything else?"

"I don't think so." Toby surveyed the interior of the compact, cube-shaped craft, which had been a gift from Professor Azareen. The roamer could travel several miles in a moment and change its own molecular structure, along with anything inside, to move through even the thickest rock wall. "We have to limit our supplies. It's a tight squeeze, even for four people." Even though the craft could adapt on the outside, the space inside couldn't be altered.

Mia sank into the pilot seat. "I thought only you, Marabella and Jurn were going on this trip."

"Yes, but we might meet someone who needs our help," Toby replied.

Gramble Horace poked his head into the door. Sweat gathered in beads above his eyebrows, which were thick and black despite his mane of white hair. "We've been fortunate; the people you have brought to join us have good intentions and are safe. But you can't read people's hearts, Toby. Be careful."

"I know." Every time Toby ventured out into the world he became more aware of people on the outside and the evil they caused. He'd been threatened just for the items in his pack. If a power-hungry individual came along and found the caverns, filled with resources meant for thousands—Toby didn't want to think about what could happen.

Jurn swung down from the ship's ceiling. His dark hair stuck out in all directions. "We can always come back if we forget something."

Gramble Horace straightened the blue bowtie he always wore no matter what endless cavern maintenance task awaited him. "Remember, this ship was designed in another world and we don't understand the technology. Even Professor Azareen isn't sure how long the ship will fly in Earth's atmosphere."

"At least we won't run out of fuel." Toby pointed out.

"Yes. We always have starlight." Gramble Horace nodded.

"And we haven't had a problem yet," Toby said.

Fear sprang into Mia's blue eyes. "But it would be horrible if something went wrong, far away, and you couldn't get home."

"True." Alone, Toby could travel through the woods quickly. His heightened cat abilities helped to sense predators and his retractable claws allowed movement through the treetops faster than any human. Any companions would slow him down and possibly be in danger.

"It'll be the last adventure for a while," he promised. "But I need to find this church."

"Most of your latest trips have gone just fine, and I understand how important this for you." Gramble Horace was the last of Toby's family who had not yet dedicated his life to Father. "But—stay safe."

"Yes, please, Toby." Mia stood up and gave him a

quick hug.

Marabella stepped in the door and smirked at Mia. "Don't worry your little fancy girl head. Jurn n' I are too mean to die."

Mia's eyes narrowed and she crossed her arms.

"And Toby is too... Trilbyish." Jurn put his hand on Toby's shoulder.

"Can't argue with that logic." Gramble Horace chuckled.

The party of three had already said goodbye to the rest of the cavern family, but Toby kept thinking of Gramble Colleen. *I'll never hug her again, at least, not for a long time.* Suddenly life seemed much more temporary.

He reached over and gave Gramble Horace a fierce hug. "I'll miss you, Gramble Horace."

Tears glistened in Gramble Horace's eyes. "Don't worry, Toby, I'll be here when you get back."

The roamer's shadow flickered over the ground, changing shape and size with the passing landscape. Toby stayed up in the sky since flying through solid objects made him queasy.

Marabella rummaged around in Jurn's tool box and picked out a battery-powered saw. "Wow, this is great!" She flicked a button and watched the blade spin.

"Give that here, you don't know how to use it." Jurn held out his hand.

Marabella switched it off and gave it back. "I bet I could work it better than you."

Jurn sighed and showed the saw to Toby. "Gramble Howard said this would be the best tool for cutting that tangled wire in the roamer's ceiling, but it just made a bunch of sparks."

"We don't even know what that alien stuff is made from, so I'm not sure what we could use. I'll look at it later." Toby pushed his hand inside a container in his armrest, where he curled and uncurled his fingers. The device used light to scan the signals and guide the ship.

He turned to see Marabella watching every motion.

She twisted a brown curl around her thumb and grinned. "Hey, Cat Kid, if anything happens to you, someone has to fly the plane, right?"

"I've taught Jurn--"

Jurn's eyes flicked to Marabella, and he frowned.

I shouldn't have said anything. After all, I was Marabella's prisoner once. She might have killed me. I can't trust her, and Jurn knows it. Toby pursed his lips into what he hoped looked like a confident smile. "This will be a quick trip. I want to meet the head of this church group. Maybe I can help them somehow."

"Why do you care about other folks anyway?" asked Marabella.

"Because it's the right thing to do." Toby pulled the view screen down closer to scan the ground. "And one of the most important commandments Father gives His children is to love each other."

"I just worry about filling my belly." Marabella bit a chunk out of an apple. "Sometimes that's all I can do." Juice dribbled down her chin.

When Toby urged the ship faster, the trees blurred into a sea of green, prickled waves. "So, we'll find this city if we follow this old highway?"

"Yes, but the forest grew up through the roads and made 'em trash." Marabella swallowed the last bite of apple core. "You know the place with those giant bridges? It takes a couple of days walking from there."

26

Toby nodded. "I passed that place before I... uh... met your group." He shook his head. *I must have looked like a scared rabbit running across the mesa while wild kids chased me.* Three years later here he was, sharing an adventure with two of those children.

A dead city passed beneath them. Though most of the buildings were completely reclaimed by the forest, a few of the tallest structures still stood defiantly in the waning light.

"No one goes into those places." Marabella pointed down to the clustered buildings. "Not even worth lookin' for loot. Some have lions and gorillers in the streets."

"Wow. I would love to see a real, live gorilla." Jurn said.

"Not today." Toby flew the craft higher.

Marabella jabbed a sticky finger towards the screen. "We're almost there. I recognize that big cliff."

The sky darkened from bright turquoise to a deep violet, and fluffy clouds gave way to stars. These were soon joined by lights from a gathering of structures on a hill in front of them.

Toby slowed the craft until it hovered over the hill. So many lights! By far the largest living city he had seen on his adventures. His ears quivered in excitement. He couldn't wait to see new faces and explore new streets. He flattened his palm and lowered it to the bottom of the container. The ship responded to his command and sank through the trees. It landed with a thud.

"You're not going to let them see your... cat stuff, are you?" Jurn frowned.

"No. At least, not at first. I don't want to scare anyone." Toby grabbed a coat from the storage bin. Dark fabric hung down to his ankles. He pulled the hood over his ears.

Jurn looked him up and down. "You sure look different! Not like Toby anymore."

"Well, that's the point, isn't it?"

"Yeah." Jurn stared at the view screen. "It's just strange."

So many times, Toby had wished his ears and tail would disappear so he could look like everyone else. Now this idea almost seemed like a betrayal.

Toby pressed a button and the door slid open. *Father, keep me safe.*

3

CITY STREETS

Toby stepped out of the roamer and into a thick stand of trees. A broken fence sprawled before him, and further on a wall peeped through the tangled forest.

The few living cities Toby had visited were all surrounded by walls of some kind, built from what materials people could scavenge. This city's walls were constructed of broken concrete, utility poles and metal sheeting. Trees had grown into cracks, widening them over time.

Why hasn't Leader come through this town? Though a year had passed since Toby had encountered the power-hungry man, he could still hear his barking voice, full of greed and hate. Yes, Leader's vehicles were too large to squeeze through the forest, but his troops could have marched in.

"You sure you don't want me to come? I have good sneak skills." Jurn surveyed the wall.

Toby shook his head. "Somebody has to guard the ship. And one can slip in easier than two."

Marabella stepped out of the cube and pointed to the left. "I got in the gate over there. Last time, nobody was watching nothin'. This city has forgotten itself."

Toby squinted to see thick metal bars of a gate, large enough for two school buses to drive through side by side. "Where's the church?"

"Not far. You havta go all the way to the end of the first street. Turn left at the blue house. The church is three buildings down from that. Has a big, white cross, the only one like it. When you get there, ask for Mr. Malachi."

Toby searched her eyes for a glint of honesty. They couldn't afford to lose the roamer, and Jurn was family to him. He had two options: take everyone home right now, or explore this new city and maybe find people who shared common goals and faith.

Marabella turned back to the ship. "Think I'll take a nap."

"Don't worry, Toby, I'll make sure she stays out of trouble," Jurn whispered.

Toby's heart urged him forward, and like usual, he chose to follow it. "All right. I won't be long." He curled his tail up under his coat.

Though Marabella said the area was deserted, Toby still moved slowly, nose in the air to catch the scent of any other creature. The hood muffled his hearing terribly, but he didn't know how these people would deal with his appearance. A teenager the size of a seven year old might be accepted. *But a Trilby?*

He slipped through the gate. It hung by one hinge, rusted and useless. Windows of buildings stared at him with empty, broken eyes. No lights glimmered in the depths.

Only stars and the crescent moon, dipped low in the sky, shed dim light on the street.

Toby crept down the first lane and found the blue house Marabella had described, though the paint was hard to see.

A creature shot out from the shadows and brushed by his legs. Just a cat, on an errand Toby could only guess, since he'd never learned how to talk to his cousins. The Trilby leaned against a wall for a moment to allow his racing heart to slow. The animal had been downwind so he hadn't scented it. He'd been too focused on finding the church to keep watch. *I must be more careful.*

He turned north. A white cross blazed in front of a building, lit up by candles flickering in windows.

For most people, the only sources of light were hand-dipped candles, a few rusted lanterns, and fires. Many chose to go to sleep with the sun. *How would these folks feel if they knew of the cavern's riches?* Toby must not reveal too much. He couldn't share information that might lead Leader to the grambles.

Scents of soap, sweat, books and... stew. A man was behind him. Toby licked his lips and turned.

The man was reaching out with a large, umber hand to touch Toby's shoulder.

"Hello, little fellow." Though soft and mellow, the man's voice still held authority. "We haven't met, and I know everyone in this town. The young, the old, and the vibrant."

"I'm a traveler, Sir." Toby tried to speak in a steady tone, but his voice shook a little. The man towered above him and could have thrown Toby against the wall as easily as a sack of flour.

The man peered down at Toby's face. "Your voice... How old are you?"

"Fifteen, Sir. I'm short."

"Well, nothing wrong with that! My name is Mr.

Malachi." The man opened his hand and pushed it closer.

"I'm Toby." He grasped the man's hand and gave what he hoped was a firm shake. "And I believe you are the reason I came to this city."

"Me?" One of Mr. Malachi's eyebrows arched up higher than the other. "Now you've got me curious, Toby. But we should go inside. Though I've helped every one of the vibrant, they'll steal what they can and you have a fancy coat. Come into the Lord's house. We will keep you sheltered."

Toby followed Mr. Malachi up the steps.

The door swung open and fingers of light and warmth reached out to usher them inside. Toby had seen pictures of grand cathedrals, giant churches and tiny chapels, all built for people of faith to come together in Father's name. But he'd never seen a church like this one. The front room opened out before him, bathed in light from lanterns and flames from a fireplace at the end of the room. A few angel statues stood in corners, and Toby could just glimpse pews and a pulpit through a door to his left.

Children milled around a long table in the center of the room, scooting chairs and clearing dishes. They laughed and chattered while they worked. Two boys rolled a ball across the room to each other while everyone else stepped around it, trying to balance dirty plates.

Mr. Malachi followed Toby's gaze. "It's the youngers' turn to clean up tonight. The olders cooked the evening meal. Busy hands make happier hearts, so we all have our duties." Malachi reached out and gently drew a child over to him. "A bored child is one of the saddest creatures in this world. Eh, Alexander?"

The candles lit up the boy's grin and revealed two missing teeth. "Yes, Mr. Malachi." He hugged the giant man and skipped off, back to work.

"A girl, Marabella, told me this city had a real church, so I came to see for myself." Toby stepped closer to the fireplace and held out his hands to the blaze.

Mr. Malachi's smile flashed. "So glad to hear the girl is safe! When she first arrived, I was sure she'd get caught up with the vibrant ones. She left the city two or three months ago and I worried for her. Few who enter the forest ever return."

He gestured to a corner by the fireplace, where roughly-hewn benches lined the walls. "Please, sit."

"What is Vibrance?" Toby took a steaming mug offered to him by a little girl.

Many of the children around him stopped and stared at the ground.

Toby frowned. "What did I say?"

"Vibrance is what used to be known as a drug," said Mr. Malachi, sitting down beside him. "Many of the children have lost family members to the Palace of Dreams, where Vibrance is made. Only the mem-keeper knows how Vibrance is made, and most of the townspeople would pay any price to walk through the palace doors, drink and forget."

A little girl with long, brown braids leaned against Mr. Malachi's shoulder and clasped her hands. "They dance there." Her soft eyes shone. "They dance to music."

"Serephina, my love, you know the dance is dangerous and steals away people's lives."

"Besides," said Alexander, who had come back to listen. "We have our own dancing times at church."

A memory of Gramble Lenora, hopping from one foot to another, head thrown back in song, made Toby smile. "We dance in our church, too."

"You go to church?" Serephina's eyes widened. "Do you have it on sunny-days?"

"Sundays?" Toby nodded. "Yep."

Malachi rose from his seat. "Children, gather around please. Chores are finished and it's time for bed. Let's bow our heads and thank the Lord for this day."

Toby knelt down while childish murmurs filled the air around him. Each child spoke their own blessing at once. *I can feel it. Father's Holy Spirit lives in this place.*

His heart was swept away to a world filled with golden light, and he heard a familiar voice, the voice of his Father say, "I love you, my son, I love you."

For a few moments after the prayer was finished, Toby kept his eyes closed. He wished the time could last forever. When he finally looked up, only Mr. Malachi remained in the room.

"Now, Toby, why don't you tell me your whole story?"

Emory blinked. A thick blanket covered his body up to his chin, and moonlight through the boarded window cast slatted shapes on the wall. He was in the healing room, a tiny alcove situated close to Mr. Malachi's quarters so a sick child could be cared for without disturbing the rest of the house.

A lantern clattered on the table by his bed and a wrinkled hand rested on his forehead. "Are you awake then, Emory, my memory?"

"Yes, Miss Jasmine, I'm awake." The nickname warmed Emory to his toes. For a long time after Sonda left he would wake up in the night, afraid the old woman had gone to the Palace. She always reassured him. "No, Dear, for you are my memory. Nothing in this world could make me happier than you."

The day's events flooded back into his mind and he

kicked the tangled blanket away from his feet. "I have to get Sonda."

"Hush, child. Malachi found you asleep in the line today. Now what if a Finder had plucked you away, like my poor Philip?" The older dabbed away a tear with a shaking hand, though her grandson had been lost before Emory was born.

"Finders haven't been out for ages, Miss Jasmine." Emory patted her hand. "Those crazies gave up a long time ago."

In the first Palace years, Finders had kidnapped children and sent them to search for mems in nearby dumps and sewers. No one bothered any more. But sometimes, when Emory passed the Palace, he almost thought he could hear children's voices join in the driving song.

"You never know." Miss Jasmine handed him a jar of water. "Vibrance has a nasty grip on people. They forget about things that didn't work and try them again."

"I need to get Sonda out of there."

"Oh, Emory, your sister always was a hardened soul. And once the Vibrance has someone, well... they almost never come back."

"I believe Sonda can be swayed." Emory took a sip of water. "I--" He suddenly remembered his elation from earlier in the day. "Oh, Miss Jasmine! I got the chopper blades to turn!"

Miss Jasmine's face sagged, causing her wrinkles to travel all the way down to the corners of her mouth. "When Mr. Malachi found that manual, I never thought you'd get such a dangerous notion into your head. What if someone finds out you have a flying machine?"

"It doesn't fly yet." Emory found his shoes and plopped down on the floor to slip them on, though they

35

were so battered, it hardly seemed worth the trouble. "I just want Sonda to see the helicopter. Maybe it will give her hope. Maybe she'll agree to come with me when I do get it finished."

"Have you lost your mind, child?" Miss Jasmine snapped. "Even if you get that thing to run, how could you ever fly it by yourself?"

"I've studied, lots." Emory grabbed his small pack and slung it over one shoulder. "I know it'll happen, because I want it so bad."

Miss Jasmine's eyelids drooped, and a tear spilled down one cheek. "How many of the children here dream about their mommies and daddies coming home? How many of the olders wish for their daughters and sons? Sisters? Brothers? The Vibrance has taken them all, and no amount of hope has ever brought them back."

"I can pray," said Emory. "Mr. Malachi came back."

The old woman's shoulders fell. "You're right. God is more powerful than the Vibrance. And He did rescue Mr. Malachi from the Dance of Dreams."

Mr. Malachi was the only person Emory knew who had been saved from the Palace after tasting the Vibrance.

"Mr. Malachi had been visiting the Palace for weeks," Miss Jasmine continued, "but his mama prayed and prayed. Then one day, he just came out. Stood in the sun and praised the Lord for his deliverance. Then he got to work, cleaning up the old church building where his parents served. And here we all are. Safe and filled with food and the Holy Spirit. So you are right, Emory. Hope remains."

The elderly woman often repeated stories, but Emory never tired of this one. He wrapped his arms around her frail waist and gave her a kiss on her cheek. "Pray for me, Miss Jasmine. I have to try."

36

4

HELP TO COME

Mr. Malachi drummed a charcoal stick against his bearded chin, seemingly oblivious to the new smudge it created with every tap. "Young friend, just by your clothes, I see you've come from a place with better resources. And you came through the forest without a scratch, so I'm guessing you have superior transportation."

Toby nodded. "Right on both counts. I can't explain too much, for my family's sake, but I wanted to see if I could be of help in some way."

Mr. Malachi sighed. "I wish you could. But word of supplies brought in would reach the Palace in an instant. Simper might pay a child or an older to be a spy for him. So far, he's left us alone, out of some distant respect, I guess. But I don't know if it would hold."

"You have a wonderful place here, Sir," Toby said.

"We welcome everyone, but we are limited by people who limit themselves." Mr. Malachi looked back at his papers, full of scrawled notes.

Toby's fingers itched to push back the hood of his

cloak. *Mr. Malachi serves Father, but what if he finds out who I really am?* Toby had encountered mixed reactions on his many journeys. Some laughed, some trembled in fear. Some accepted him without question. *What would Mr. Malachi think?* A sharp pang of doubt made his head ache. *I'll worry about it later.*

"Is there another way I could be of use to you? Maybe we could bring a doctor in every couple of months. Or some new books." Toby's eyes flickered over the contents of the room. Though clean and well-kept, the furniture and other items were either half a century old or handmade from recycled or raw materials. *Just a few tools from the caverns could make life so much easier for these people.*

Mr. Malachi's eyes lit up. "It's hard to refuse new books." He shook his head. "But it's too dangerous."

"Then maybe I could take someone back with me?"

Mr. Malachi stared down at the sheets of yellowed paper covering his lap. "No. I don't think anyone here will leave family members who are in the Palace. These papers contain my prayer requests, and the names of everyone in town. I read through them every day to remind myself of what has been answered and what I still need to pray about. I do have a task you could probably manage, but I hesitate to ask a child for something so dangerous."

Toby straightened his shoulders. "Sir, I haven't been a child for a long time."

"Of course. I keep forgetting."

"How can I be of service?" Toby pressed. "Does someone need to be rescued?"

"All who enter the Palace need salvation." Mr. Malachi picked up a glass jar. "Water is our most precious resource. A river still courses through an old drainage network under the city. We collect the water in tanks and pass it through a filtration system so no one has to venture into the forest."

"That's good." Toby was impressed.

"Yes. But even through this rainy season, the water supply has been halved, then halved again. We believe something has blocked the flow. A system is in place to collect rain, but it's not enough. We've checked every accessible route, but right before the Palace of Dreams a giant metal fence blocks the way. We don't have the tools to pry it open. Someone has to go through the Palace and see if there's a way down into the tunnels."

"What makes you think I can get inside?" Toby asked.

"Simper will not be able to resist two things. You are a new customer." Malachi pulled a small golden cross from around his neck and held it out to Toby. "And you will offer him my last memory."

Toby hesitated. "Surely we could give something else."

"No, this is fine." Mr. Malachi dropped the necklace into Toby's hands and closed the Trilby's fingers over it. "My mamma wore it every day. Right before she died, she gave it to me. She said, 'Son, you have to know when to hold on, and you have to know when to surrender something to the Lord.' I thought she was talking about her own soul, but now I can see she meant... well, everything in this world."

"Why does Simper care so much about memories anyway?"

Mr. Malachi leaned back in his chair. "Back in my younger days, Simper was on the town council. Our city was doing fairly well; survivors of the disaster came in from other places to join us. But a terrible sickness struck the area, and many people died, including Simper's family. All of their personal belongings, including their home, had to be burned."

"How terrible," Toby said. "So he collects other people's things?"

Mr. Malachi nodded. "Because he doesn't have any more memories of his own. His sanity and reason were lost in the fire."

Toby held the cross until it warmed in his hand, then put it in his pocket. "I think I'm going to need some help. I have a friend waiting for me outside of the wall who is, well, taller. I'd feel safer going in with someone else."

"I will send my prayers along with you." Mr. Malachi said. "I'm grateful you would risk your safety to help out our city."

"I hope we can find out what's wrong. We'll do our very best."

Heavy raindrops splashed on Emory's cheeks as he approached the Palace. The mourners had disappeared. Only one person leaned against the wall under an awning. Her head lolled a little to the side and her sleeves covered her hands like knobby mittens.

"Sonda..." his heart skipped a beat. "Oh, Sonda, you're out!"

"Hey, Emory." A slow smile pulled at the corners of his sister's white, rubbery lips. Hair hung in limp strands over her shoulders.

When was the last time she had cared for herself? Vibrance users lost all sense of day and night. They only left the Palace when the mem-keeper deemed their memory spent and sent them out the door to find another.

"Hey, got any mems?" Sonda leaned closer. Her eyes darted in and out of focus.

"You've taken everything, Sonda."

Her claw-like hand reached out and grabbed his wrist.

Blue liquid trickled from the corner of his sister's mouth and a sickly-sweet scent hit his nose.

"Come on, Emory, I need something! You never gave me a birthday present!"

Her fifteenth birthday had been last week, but even if Emory could have scrounged up some tiny gift, he'd never give her a way to buy Vibrance.

"Hurry up, I want to go back inside." She laughed with her mouth wide open, then muffled it with her hand. "Oh, the dance was such fun tonight!"

Emory's head reeled, and a queasy feeling crept into his stomach, but he took his sister's hand.

"Sonda, listen. I might have a way out of here. If you'll just follow me, I'll show you..."

"A way out? You found mems?" Sonda squeezed his fingers. "Emory, how wonderful!" She glanced at his pockets, then his pack. "Where did you put them?"

"No, not mems..." Emory looked back over his shoulder. The street was deserted. "Look, come with me." He pulled her down the street, past a few buildings, where two battered dumpsters sagged together.

"Emory, what on earth... why'd you bring me back here?"

"It's a secret. No one else can know, Sonda. You gotta promise."

Sonda slouched against a post. "Okay, whatever. But you'd better have some mems."

"No, Sonda, not mems." Emory's voice rose in his excitement. "I fixed up a flying machine. We might be able to get away from here!"

Feet crunched glass on the street behind him, and he was yanked around to face a tall, thin person.

"What'ya buggin' Sonda about today, Brat?"

The light of dawn dusted the early morning raindrops away and coaxed the squirrels out into the forest. They chattered amongst themselves and scampered off when Toby passed.

A cold hand of fear tightened around Toby's throat. *What if the roamer was gone?* A journey on foot back to the Grambles' cavern would take at least a week, if no incident slowed him down. *Which never happens.* And he couldn't leave Jurn.

The roamer shimmered into view a few hundred yards away. The panel slid open, and Jurn popped out. "Hi! I decided to move over a little ways just in case."

Toby sank against a tree in relief. "I thought the ship was gone!" He stumbled into the cube and glanced around. "Where's Marabella?"

Jurn's face darkened. "She tried to get me to steal the ship, Toby. Should've known I would never leave you here."

"Did she fight you?"

"No." Jurn wiped a speck of dust off the pilot's seat. "Marabella said sooner or later Leader would find you, and she'd rather be on the winning side. I thought I'd talked her out of leaving by the time she went to sleep. I really tried to keep my eyes open, Toby. But well, when I woke up, she'd gone."

Toby's heart sank. "Do you think she'll tell him where we are?"

"Nope. She wouldn't get me and Tinga into trouble." Jurn grinned. "Gosh, good thing Gramble Lenora can't see your face. You're filthy!"

Toby sat down hard in his seat. Should he pursue Marabella, try to reason with her? How far away was

Leader? Leader had already found out about Toby. Worst of all, he knew Toby possessed technology far surpassing the vehicles the man's band had managed to patch together.

Toby rubbed his eyes and yawned. "I found the church. The pastor asked us to help them." He explained to Jurn about the palace and the water problem.

"He really thinks we can find out what's wrong?" Jurn asked. "Seems like he's putting a lot of faith in two strange kids."

Toby nodded. "Yes, but he's desperate. We'd have to go today. Mr. Malachi is worried the water flow could stop at any time. The whole city is hanging by a thread and if the supply is gone they won't survive."

"But what about Marabella?" Jurn protested.

"If you're convinced she won't tell on us, we might still have time. Leader's vehicles move on rubber tires filled with air. One puncture and the whole caravan is crippled. And we might be worried about nothing. No one's found the Grambles, not for forty-five years." Toby put his hands over his face. "Except Marabella. Ugh."

Jurn stared at him. "You're still worried, aren't you?"

Toby looked down. "Our safety rests in Father's hands. Would he bring us this far, just to let us go now?"

"I hope not."

"Me too." Toby pulled his hood over his ears. "Let's go and see if we can help Mr. Malachi."

The grip on Emory's shoulder tightened as the man pulled him through the city streets. Emory tried to wrench away and received a slap on the side of his head that almost knocked him down.

"Don't hurt him, Stance!" Sonda ran beside them, wringing her hands. A glimmer of fear shone through the haze of Vibrance in her eyes. "Stance, come on, he's my brother!"

"Uh-huh. I bet he knows how ta get more mems!"

Sonda tripped over a pile of loose bricks, recovered, and fell back into step. "Emory, is that true? Did you find mems?"

Stance shoved Emory against a wall. Sharp stones dug into Emory's back.

"Look, boy," Stance hissed. "You'd better take us to this... machine, and quick. I'm outta trinkets and I need more. Used to, we could find 'em. Closets, grates, warehouses. The rat-filled, nasty places no one would check. But Simper has almost everything now, underground, I'm betting. Can't even get an old photo anymore."

Emory's lips parted, and the secret he shared with only a few of the olders almost slipped out. Rooms under the floors of God's Shelter Church held shelves and shelves of books, papers and magazines. Over two thousand volumes were kept there, and if the mem-keeper found out, he would send the Vibrance users to the church to take them. A book could buy you a week at the Palace, especially if it had pictures.

The boy pressed his mouth closed. The library was worth more than his safety, or even rescuing his sister. Once the olders died, the books would be the only record of the world before the disaster. "To learn from our mistakes," he whispered.

"What was that?" Stance leaned closer.

Emory pulled in a breath of air and let out a gusty sigh. He almost expected to see his hopes fall to the ground like a pile of feathers. "I can show you the machine, but it's not ready to fly. I still have to work on a few things."

"Emory, don't you see?" Sonda wheedled. "We don't have time for that. We need mems right now, today."

Stance yanked Emory back out into the street and pushed him forward. "I'm guessing your machine's in a building outside of town. The last of the cars and trucks were pulled apart years ago, when I was a little boy."

"Yes." Emory gasped. "I found a place no one opened, I don't know why. I guess the razor wire kept people out. I got through and you can too."

Away he led them, from the safety of Mr. Malachi, but also from the temptation of the precious books. It would have been so much easier to show Stance the library. Perhaps in the chaos that followed, he and Sonda could have slipped away...

Never. Maybe the helicopter would fly today. Stance would just have to go with them. And perhaps the people in the new city would know how to help Stance too.

5

ROOFTOP REWARDS

Miss Jasmine led Toby and Jurn through the center of the church building. Rosy hues of dawn blended with patterned light from stained glass windows.

Toby drank in the multi-colored images. Peter and the Apostles. Jesus at the Last Supper. Miraculously preserved while desperation and anger shifted through the world outside. *Respect is still reserved for churches, though few people follow Father.* Peace blanketed the building.

This feeling followed Toby, while the group went up two flights of stairs and out on the roof.

Mr. Malachi stood by a large metal tank and directed children while they carried buckets of water to various patches of earth. Plants sprawled over fences in areas, while a few plots were covered with old boards or metal scraps.

"I wanted you to see why our water is so precious." Mr. Malachi turned to Toby. "We have sustained these rooftop gardens and farms for decades." He pointed to a cluster of cages on an adjoining roof. "Many plants came from original seeds, and most animals are descendants of livestock before the disaster. Some were scavenged from the forest. If our water runs dry, all could be lost."

The animal pens housed goats, chickens and even forest animals. Squirrels scurried in cages, and deer stood at fences to search passing hands for food. *Like the underground farms in the caverns.* "People have such an amazing will to survive, no matter what," Toby murmured.

Mr. Malachi's eyes rested on Jurn. "How old are you, boy?"

"He's twelve." Toby glanced up at his friend. "But he looks older. I trust him with my life."

Jurn stood a little straighter. "I'll do what I can to help, sir."

Mr. Malachi chuckled. "I believe it. Sadly, they allow twelve year olds to dance in the Palace. Especially if you offer an object with a memory like the one I gave to Toby."

"They let kids my age use that Vibrance stuff?" Jurn shook his head.

A small hand tugged on Mr. Malachi's shirt. "I need you."

Mr. Malachi bent down to the little girl's level. "What is it, Seraphina?"

"Emory, Sir. After he woke up, he went back out to find his sister. Ed n' Edith saw him being pushed down the alley by Stance. Toward the warehouses."

Mr. Malachi sighed. "I should never have given him that repair manual!"

"What's going on?" asked Toby.

"One of the boys here, Emory, has a sister in the Palace," said Mr. Malachi. "He found an old flying machine, and he's been trying to get it to work again. I figured no harm could be done, sometimes a spark of hope can keep people alive longer than a storehouse of medicine.

But if Stance finds it... he's a bad one."

Mr. Malachi knelt down and touched Serephina's quivering chin. "Don't worry, I'll go after the boy. Spread the news, no one leaves the building until I return." He glanced over at Toby. "You and Jurn go with Miss Jasmine. She'll explain everything you need to know about the Palace."

Miss Jasmine smiled and beckoned for them to follow her again. When she turned to leave, her hair puffed out around her shoulders, just like Gramble Colleen.

Toby choked back a sudden sob. *I have to keep it together. I can't help these people if I'm focused on my own sadness.*

He tucked his grief in an imaginary box at the back of his mind and followed Miss Jasmine down the stairs.

Emory's hands shook while he pried apart the fence. Lack of sleep made it hard to concentrate on his task.

Sonda leaned against a tree with her eyes closed, and Stance made no move to help either. "Hurry up, unless you want another slap."

"I'm trying!" Emory propped the section back and scooted under it. "Come on."

Sonda squeezed through, then Stance, who cursed every rock and stick.

Emory picked his way through the brush.

Stance caught up with Emory and smacked the back of his head. "Hurry up."

Emory calculated hours in his mind while stumbling forward. The effects of Vibrance didn't last long. *When it wears off, things are gonna get worse.* He worked his way over to the side panel and pushed it open.

Stance scratched a fresh insect bite. "This better be

worth it, you little nit."

"Oh, Emory," Sonda breathed when she saw the helicopter. Her eyes shone.

Maybe she understands now! Emory's heart filled with joy. "Let me show you!" He swung up into the cabin, threw switches and pushed up the lever.

Nothing happened.

His sister's face still held its bright smile. "Well?"

He ran through the list again in his mind while yanking at switches and pulling levers he had never even touched. *Am I doing it wrong?* Something had to be loose, or maybe a mouse got to the wires.

"Uh, I need to fix some things, very small. Might take me a few hours."

"A few hours?" Stance pushed his way up to the pilot area. His stinking breath poured into Emory's face. "I don't have time for that! I need mems now!" His head snapped from side to side like a snake as he surveyed the interior of the helicopter. "Hey, Sonda, you should come in here. I bet the mem-keeper might like some of these shiny buttons. And look at this fancy seat!"

Sonda poked her head in. Her usually sallow cheeks were tinged with pink. "Oh, Stance, we're rich!"

Stance grabbed a screwdriver from the instrument panel where Emory had left it the day before. "Hey, help me pry off this metal thingy."

"No!" Emory threw himself in front of the controls. "Can't you see? This machine could get us away from here!"

Sonda stared at him. "Leave the Palace? Why we would we want to do that?" He pushed the screwdriver towards Emory's face. "Now get outta my way, unless you wanna lose an eye."

Emory's heart dropped.

A loud, metallic sound came from the side of the warehouse. Emory froze. Shadowy figures approached the helicopter. Two, then five more.

"Stance, is that you?" An older man stared up at them. Most of his teeth were broken down to his pale gums.

"Find something?" A woman stepped into the light. "You wasn't gonna keep it from the rest of us, was ya?"

The next events shot past Emory like bullets. Stance and Sonda shoved Emory aside and began to hammer and yank at the instrument panel. Even while Emory begged them to stop, more people swarmed the machine.

Emory's pack was ripped from his shoulders, and rough fingers tore through his pockets. He was pushed, pinched and slapped until he tumbled to the warehouse floor. Through the helicopter's windows, hands tore into upholstery, wires and fiberglass panels.

He watched his last hope disappear like a warm breath in winter's air. Emory crawled to a dark corner of the warehouse and cried.

A man opened the door and leaned heavily against it. Thick spidery veins filled the whites of his eyes. Toby was used to people towering above him but this man was even taller than Mr. Malachi and wavered like he might topple over at any moment.

"What d'ya want? We don't let in children under the age of twelves. Youngers can't take the Vibrance, kills 'em dead." The tiniest point of the man's tongue stuck out of the corner of his mouth when he talked, and gave his words a slobbery sound.

Toby shuddered. The grambles never drank. He had only seen examples of substance abuse in movies.

Disgusted as he felt, this man held the fate of their mission in his hands.

"I'm fifteen, sir." He stretched as tall as possible. "I'm just small for my... I'm just small."

"Yeah, like I never heard that one before." The man's beefy hand reached around for the outside doorknob to draw it back.

Jurn stepped forward. "Look, sir, we're both old enough. We want to see Mr. Simper."

"Mr. Simper, eh?" A crafty look spread over the man's face. "Wouldn't be you have something of value in those teensy pockets?" He stepped outside and closed the door behind him. "Well, why don't we see what you got."

Toby itched to cover the pocket holding the gold cross, but he kept his hands folded together. "We will wait to see Mr. Simper, with all due respect." He tried to keep his tone cheerful, but it ended with a bit of a hiss.

"Is that so?" The man reached behind him for a stick propped up against the wall. "Well, I'm good as him. I can take it in, you see? Then I'll come back and tell you what he thinks." He smacked the rod against his hand. "If it's something good, maybe you'll get luckier next time."

"Scaring my customers, Mitts?" A voice, cold as old bones, grated through the doorway.

Toby's hands relaxed. The relief on Jurn's face mirrored his own feelings.

Another man stepped out on the porch, the type of person who wouldn't be noticed on the street; not tall nor short; thick nor thin. His clothes and hair were a drab, ordinary gray.

Then he gazed down at Toby, and his eyes burned like molten silver. Bright and sharp, in no way muddled. The look pierced Toby's soul.

Simper.

Toby stepped forward. "We have a memory for you, Sir. We wish to gain admittance to the Palace of Dreams."

Simper raised a hand to usher them inside. "Come in, boys, come in!"

Another tremor ran through Toby, almost like he was walking into his own grave.

Mitts smiled a toothless grin. "Welcome to the Palace."

6

Emory huddled in the corner, eyes shut tight long after the pops, shuffles and shouts died away. He still couldn't quite believe what had just happened. *Maybe if I wish hard enough, I can go back in time and everything will be right again.*

Then he heard new steps, in long sure strides. He opened his eyes.

"Are you hurt?" Mr. Malachi kneeled down by the boy.

Emory shook his head.

"Good. I got here as quickly as I could. Son, let's go home." Mr. Malachi bent down and offered him his hand.

Emory rose on trembling legs and surveyed the warehouse. Pieces of foam from the helicopter's seats littered the floor, and pages of his repair manual danced in the breeze like dried leaves. He couldn't face the inside of the helicopter, so he simply turned and walked out into the yard.

Hot tears slipped down his cheeks again. "How could they be so stupid?" His hands clenched into fists.

Mr. Malachi scooped him up into a hug. Emory could feel the big man's heart thumping under the soft material of his shirt.

"Emory, my son, 'Even the youth grow tired and faint,

but He brings strength to those who wait.' That's from the Bible. We must trust God has a better plan."

Emory wiped his nose on his sleeve. "But how do I know for sure?"

"Because the Bible says 'He makes all things work together for the good of those who love Him.'"

"But what about Sonda? She doesn't love anything but Vibrance."

Mr. Malachi squeezed under the fence, then helped Emory. "Sometimes we have to hold up other people with our faith when they don't have any for themselves. Don't give up. Your sister might still be saved."

Toby and Jurn followed Simper down a hallway while Mitt lumbered behind them. Darkness covered the walls on either side, but when Toby stretched out a hand, his fingertips ran along a series of cracks. His shoes scuffed over threadbare carpet.

Simper opened a door before them, and they stepped into a clean, sunlit room. Paintings of waterfalls and forests covered the tan walls . A lone desk surrounded by chairs sat in the middle of the space. Stacks of paper and a glass jar filled with pencils and pens rested on the glossy desk surface.

Jurn's eyebrows traveled up to his snarled bangs.

"Boys, let me explain how things work here at the Palace." Simper perched on a chair and gestured for the boys to sit in the seats across from him. "Payments come into this room only. So let's see what you have." He pulled out a blank sheet of paper from the stack and an ancient pencil from the jar. "Since it's your first time, I'll give you an extra day, and all the Vibrance you can handle, of course."

"Won't be much, I can tell you that!" Mitts guffawed behind them.

"You can go now." Simper didn't even glance up at the big man.

Mitt's mouth pulled down at the corners like an angry bulldog, but he turned and walked out of the room. He left the door cracked behind him.

"Close it all the way, Mitts." Simper's voice never rose.

The door slammed shut.

Simper looked up from his paper expectantly.

"Oh, yes. Here." Toby brought out the cross. The gold gleamed in the streaks of sun coming from the windows.

"Bless me!" A grin of pure greed flicked across Simper's face for a tiny second, then his mouth drew back into its normal stoic expression. "Yes, yes, boy, the trinket will do. Always wait for me before you reveal the treasure, remember that."

He picked up the pencil. "Necklace will buy you three days for two. Then a free day, so... four."

And we only need one. Toby let out a sigh of relief. "Thank you, Mr. Simper." He signed his name under the contract the man had hastily scribbled.

Simper held out his hand, and Toby dropped in the necklace. Thin, gray fingers closed around the gold. "The Palace is right through that door, boys. Wonder! Delight! The dance of forgetfulness!"

Jurn walked out.

Toby followed and shut the door. Then he stuck his head back inside. "Mr. Simper, what is the Vibrance made from?"

The man sprang up from the floor behind the desk, banging his head. He moved to the door with surprising swiftness for a man of his age and slammed it in Toby's face, but not before Toby noticed the rug under the desk had been pulled back.

"Okay, never mind." Toby said to the closed door. *I bet he has a secret under that desk.*

Toby turned and squinted. The size of the room was obscured by darkness, but the place was hot and stuffy, and smelled of mold and candle wax. No windows brought in light.

A group of musicians stood on a raised platform on the room's edge. One man blew through the mouthpiece of a brass horn or tuba, attached to a yellowed plastic pipe. Another beat on a row of rusty pots and pans with two bent spoons. A woman strummed strings stretched over part of a bicycle frame.

Dozens of bare feet slapped the ground and added to the bizarre melody. Men and women danced with no apparent pattern or purpose. Some jerked and moved erratically, while some stood in one spot and swayed, looks of pure bliss on their pale, thin faces.

An eerie blue light settled over everything.

Shelves lined the walls, and on these sat rows and rows of small glass jars filled with a blue liquid. Toby realized candles behind the glass were casting the light.

A woman lurched out of the group and staggered towards one of the shelves. She grasped a jar with an unsteady hand and drank the liquid down in one gulp.

A darting shape moved from the shadows. A person took the jar just emptied by the woman and replaced it with a full one. "A fresh one, here, Sir." A child's face, almost level with Toby's, peered into his hood.

"But, you're so young," Toby said. "I thought kids under twelve weren't allowed into the Palace."

"Most aren't, only us special ones." The boy squared thin shoulders and ran a hand through his thick, shaggy hair. "We are the Vibrance keepers. We help the Palace run good, then we earn a free month of dancing when we're old enough. I only got one year left 'til my time."

"You really want to be like them?" Toby nodded toward the stumbling group of dancers. One man had passed out on the floor. The other people paid him no mind, just danced around him. Some tripped over his inert form.

Several children came forward and carried him out of the way, gently placing him on a mat by the wall.

"Oh, yes." The boy gazed at the dancers with a small smile on his lips. "Don't you see? They can't remember."

"Vibrance really makes people forget things?"

"Yes." The boy clutched the jar to his chest. "Ma died when I was five, and then my brother. I tried to make the hurt go away for so long. It just don't. But Vibrance is like magic. Makes you forget all of your heart pains."

Toby stared at the blue liquid. Memories of Gramble Colleen ached so much, like splinters stuck into his heart. And the people he had met, the ones who would not accept help. Their faces haunted him every night. Maybe a tiny sip of Vibrance could numb the pain.

"Toby! What are you doing?" Jurn hissed beside him.

Toby whipped around. "Uh, just looking at the Vibrance. I was um, trying to figure out what it is. It's such a weird color, right?"

He bent down to get a closer look. A man lurched to the table, reaching for a jar. The man tripped and caught Toby's shoulder to keep from falling.

Toby's hood slipped down.

The room grew silent. Several children paused from their jobs, mouths hanging open. A few of the dancers moved closer. They stared at... his ears.

"Oh no," he breathed.

Mitts slunk out of the shadows where he had been watching them. "Hmmm, what have we here? I had a feeling I needed to keep an eye on you. What kinda monster are you, boy?"

"I'm not a monster! I just--" Toby's normal explanation died on his tongue. *It's no use.* These were not reasonable people.

"Everyone in the Palace knows ya don't hide stuff from me." Mitts grabbed Toby's arm and pulled him towards the door. "I'm gonna show you my closet."

Jurn's terrified eyes followed Toby all the way to the door.

Toby mouthed, "Go back to Malachi." He could only hope his friend understood the message in the dim light.

By the time Emory and Malachi reached the church, the boy's sobs had settled into an occasional hiccup or sniffle.

Malachi murmured a few words of comfort and then fell silent.

Emory wondered how his heart could still beat, after being cracked into tiny pieces. *Nothing will make it better.*

The front room of the church was deserted when they entered. Most youngers would be on the roof or preparing the mid-day meal in the kitchen. A breakfast of bread and one potato for each of them had been left on the table.

"I hope Toby's all right." Mr. Malachi said as they sat down.

Emory gripped the now-cold potato for a moment, then hurled it at an angel statue. The vegetable burst into sticky fragments, and the sculpture rocked on its base. Yellow bits dropped off a marble cheek.

The bread would have followed, but Mr. Malachi gently pried it from his hand and set it on the plate. "Your anger is understood, but let's not waste precious food or threaten one of our few remaining pieces of art."

"Sorry," muttered Emory, but he didn't feel sorry. Even his anger was gone now, hurled away along with the potato. In its place was a hollow void of nothingness... no pain, no sorrow. No hope.

"My poor boy." Mr. Malachi's forehead rippled with the wrinkles that only appeared when he was most concerned. "We've lost so many people dear to us. Like my family. And your parents, whom I loved like a brother and sister. But Emory, we cannot lose our hope."

"What if there's nothing left to hope for?" Emory thought he had cried himself dry, but new tears burned the corners of his eyes.

Malachi's eyes twinkled. "Child, we always have hope. Just remember, we're in this world for what seems like a blink of an eye, and then we'll be with Jesus. Until then, we cannot give up on His work."

Emory remembered the good times, when his parents were alive. One autumn day, they had all been up on the roof working together. Though covered in dirt and sweat, all were happy. The harvest promised to be a bountiful one and everyone's belly would be full all winter.

His father had hoisted him up on his strong, broad shoulders, and Sonda had skipped along with her hand wrapped in the colorful material of their mother's skirt. The family stood on the edge of the roof and watched the bright circle of sun settle lazily into the horizon.

He missed the childish security, the knowledge his family would always be close by to surround him with safety and love. The memory was a scrap in his mind threatening to blow away with every fresh disappointment.

"Hoping makes me tired." Emory settled his head into the crook of his arm.

"So does staying up for most of the night." Malachi patted his hand. "Try to take a nap while I keep watch for the boys who are trying to help us.."

The door burst open, and Serephina flew inside. Shouts and screams were cut off when she slammed the door behind her. "Fight... at the Palace," she gasped.

"Not again!" Mr. Malachi sprang to his feet. "Emory, you stay here and get some rest. I'd better make sure our new friends are safe."

7

UNDERNEATH

The closet was exactly what it sounded like: a small, narrow room, filled with so much junk Toby couldn't move without stepping on something sharp or squishy. A tiny window near the ceiling kept the room from going completely black when Mitt slammed the door. Toby heard the rasp of a bolt, angry clunks as Mitt stomped down the flight of stairs they had come up, and then... nothing.

Toby examined the wall. The same pattern of cracks he remembered from the hallway covered the plaster here. *Maybe I can break through the wall.* He peeled away a handful of white powdery chunks before he hit solid wood

A rummage through the piles of junk turned up splintered boards, wads of cloth and some broken jars. *Wow. I'd better not cut myself.*

He finally cleared a space big enough to settle down and think. A few years ago, if Toby had found himself in such a horrible situation, he might have cried. But after all his adventures he'd learned no matter how dark or desperate the place, he was never alone.

"Father, I'm sorry for letting the Vibrance tempt me. I have to let you reach in and heal my hurts. I don't understand why you allowed me to be captured like this, but I trust you. Please, please help me."

Since he didn't have a watch and no view of the sky to chart the sun's course, he could only judge the passage of time by his grumbling stomach.

A shaft of sunlight settled on his upturned face, and he squinted up at the window.

How strong is that glass? He rose and picked his way through the piles of stuff until he stood by the wall. Mitts would never consider the window a means of escape. Nothing in the closet would be sturdy enough to stand on, and the ledge was far too high for a normal person to reach.

But I'm a Trilby! Toby dug through the junk until he found a part of a broom handle. He wrapped a cloth around the wooden stick and clenched it between his teeth. Then he stuffed his gloves in his coat pocket and extended his claws. Sharp points dug through the plaster and into the wood beneath the window with little effort. He hoisted himself up a few feet, gripped the surface with his soft shoes and quickly scaled the wall to the window. Toby grasped the window sill with one hand and held the stick in the other. One good smack and the glass shattered. Then he placed the cloth over the jagged glass and crawled into the open air.

Toby scooted across the ledge and looked down. Beneath him was the entrance to the Palace, where Simper had greeted them earlier.

Mitt's bald head shone below. Toby was tempted, like most boys would be, to hit the target with a spit ball.

A few fragments of glass gleamed on the concrete

around Mitts. Amazingly, the man hadn't seemed to notice.

Leafy branches shaded the porch and reached almost to Toby's perch. The tree would provide the perfect means of escape, but not with Mitts so close. *I need a distraction. What can I do to get him away from the door?*

Mitts stared down the street and put up a hand to shield his head from sun spotting through the branches.

Toby's ears swiveled. A crowd of people approached from a distant lane.

Simper's gray head bobbed over the threshold to join Mitts. His dry voice floated up. "What's going on?"

"Some kinda fight, I guess, Boss." Mitts turned back to the door. "I'm going in to do that thing... I need ta' finish."

Simper pulled him back around. "Nice try. You're coming with me to find out what's going on." He rubbed his hands together. "Maybe someone found a treasure. We'd better hurry, I don't want it damaged."

"Thank you, Father!" Toby prayed as the two men disappeared in the direction of the crowd noises.

He waited another minute, then leapt to the nearest branch. His claws slipped on the smooth bark, but then caught and held firm. He hung for an instant, then wrapped his body around the limb. Branch by branch, he worked his way down to the ground.

A quick look around. No one nearby. He darted to the door. In the rush to discover the loot headed his way, Simper had failed to remove the key from the lock. One twist and Toby was in.

Through the darkened hall again. Into the lighted office. Toby rushed to the desk and flipped back the rug beneath it.

I knew it. A trap door cut into the wood, with a metal ring in the center. *This has to lead to Simper's hoard.* Toby wasn't interested in random treasures, but it might have an entrance to the water system as well.

"Toby," a voice whispered.

He dropped the rug and scrambled up the back of a chair.

"Didn't mean to scare you." Jurn grinned.

Toby wiped sweat off his forehead. "I have to stop letting my curiosity distract me from keeping watch!"

"Aw, I'm good at sneaking. Hey, where did that mean guy lock you up, anyway? How'd you get out?"

"Tell you later." Toby picked up the rug again. "Look what I found."

Jurn stared at the door. "Can you move it?"

Toby grabbed the ring, but Jurn had to help him pull up the solid wooden panel and place it to the side.

Jurn pulled a flashlight from his pocket. "Shall we?"

"Isn't that my flashlight?" Toby eyed the device.

Jurn shrugged. "Yeah, you left it in the roamer."

"Would have come in handy a few minutes ago."

"Uh-huh." Jurn made no move to return the flashlight, just snapped it on and shone the light down in the hole.

"There's a ladder here, but I can't see the bottom." Toby peered down into the darkness.

"Hopefully there's no gorillas down there," Jurn said.

"Yeah, that might be bad."

The two boys descended into the darkness.

Toby drummed the ladder rung in an impatient rhythm. Jurn could only use one hand because of the flashlight, and he did not have Toby's climbing skills. "Jurn, we need to hurry. Simper and Mitts will come back and find the door open."

Jurn turned his face up, blinking when dust blew into his eyes. "Well, we couldn't exactly close it behind us! This whole idea is crazy."

I know. Toby stepped down, rung by rung, as soon as

Jurn's hands moved further below him.

Toby reached the bottom and shivered in the sudden chill. "All right, let me have my flashlight."

Jurn handed it over.

Toby swept the room with light.

This area was a true cavern, hollowed out by thousands of years of flowing water, just like the caves Toby had lived in for his first twelve years.

"Wow!" breathed Jurn.

Rows and rows of shelves, cabinets and other furniture lined the wall. Jewelry, photographs, dishes, and figurines covered every surface. The cavern storage areas in Toby's home held useful things, tools and beds and tents, items to aid in survival. The trinkets surrounding him were objects people valued because they brought back...

"Memories." A knick-knack caught Toby's eye, and he picked the item up and held it to the light. A craftsman from long ago had shaped the blue glass into the form of a small bird. It seemed miraculous that something so delicate and fragile could survive decades of violence. *Mia would love this bird.* He placed it back on the shelf. To take the figurine would be stealing. *Besides, I'd never get it home in one piece.*

"What's this, Toby?" Jurn held up a large ball with hundreds of mirrors embedded in its surface. The surfaces reflected the light from the flashlight, causing tiny rainbows to dance over the shelves.

Toby looked back from the wall. "I think it's a disco ball. Come on, Jurn, I found a door. We don't have time to look at this stuff. The town's water supply is far more valuable."

A row of deadbolts were embedded in the door. "Good thing we can open these from this side." Toby slid them out, one by one. "Hopefully we can find the water source through here."

Jurn pulled himself away from the mounds of treasure and joined Toby. "Or Simper could trap us if there's not another way out."

"We'll be caught for sure if we go back up the ladder. We just have to take the chance." Toby pushed open the door.

Toby's shoes slid as the ground tipped sharply and then ended on a ledge. His head spun a little when he looked over the side. They were standing eighty, maybe a hundred feet up on the edge of a giant tunnel. Below them, a wide river ran through the cavern.

Torches in the walls lit up the other bank of the river, where dozens of children milled around. Because of the distance, Toby couldn't tell what they were doing, but the kids seemed focused and organized.

"Can you believe this is all under the Palace?" Jurn whispered behind him.

"The ground keeps secrets well. No one would ever guess the grambles' caverns were there, just by standing above them," Toby replied. "We'd better figure out how to get down to the bottom before anyone sees us."

"Climb down?" Jurn's face turned white. "From here?"

Toby pointed to a narrow path, carved into the side of the wall. "I think that's the route, over there."

"Yeah, looks like a great way for *you*." Jurn flattened himself back against the wall.

"Aw, it's a piece of cake." Toby swung himself over the ledge and landed on the path. "The climb isn't too steep. I'll help you."

They crept down. Every placement of hand or foot had to be thought out. A loose stone might betray their presence or cause them to plunge to their deaths.

"Toby, I don't know if I can do this." Jurn's eyes were squeezed shut, and he trembled.

"Jurn, we're half way down. Do you want to get closer to the ground or go back up higher?"

Jurn opened his eyes and began to move again with tiny steps.

Toby could see what the kids were doing now. Some of them swiped the sides of the cavern wall with thin, flat boards, collecting a slimy substance to dump into jars. A separate team of children took the filled jars. Toby couldn't quite see the process but it looked like they were filtering the goop to mix with water in jars. These finished jars were then carried through another door Toby assumed must lead to the Palace.

Of course there's another exit. Simper would never let the children into his treasure room.

"I wonder they are gathering and mixing with the water?" Toby said.

"I think this might be it." Jurn pulled a piece of moss from a crack in the rocks. "It looks different when it's dry like this, but I bet when you mix it with water it gets all slimy. It's the same color."

How had Simper found this place and learned how to make the moss into Vibrance?

A grating noise came from above them.

"What was that?" Jurn looked up. Cracks snaked through the rock ceiling.

Screams erupted from the other side of the river, and children darted up the banks like minnows fleeing from a shark.

A huge piece of rock crashed to the ground below, exploding into fragments and dust.

8

LIGHT AT THE END

"Was anyone hurt?" Toby strained to see through the white dust settling on the rocks below.

"Don't think so." Jurn pointed toward faces peeking out from openings in the wall.

"The ceiling is full of holes. The kids are probably used to rocks falling." Toby frowned. "I think we're still under the Palace. No wonder the walls are so cracked. It's amazing the whole place didn't fall through the ground years ago. Simper has to know of the danger, why does he still let people come in?"

They finally reached the bottom of the cliff. Toby darted across an open area and crouched behind a boulder.

Jurn followed, but tripped on a rock and rolled in the dust. He lay there for a moment, holding his knee and grimacing.

He crawled over to Toby and settled in, saying words under his breath he would never have used around the grambles.

"Are you all right?" Toby flashed the light on Jurn's knee. The cloth was torn and a small spot of blood soaked through.

"Yes," Jurn sighed. "I'm just glad to be done with that climb. Let's keep moving."

A trickle of rocks bounced down the wall from the ledge. Toby thought for a moment that another boulder had loosened, but a gravelly voice from above shouted out, "Children, spies have invaded our cave. Find them!"

Toby froze. *Where can we go now?*

"The river flows into town, so we might be able to find a way out if we follow the current," he whispered to Jurn.

Jurn nodded and they scampered down along the rock bank, slipping and sliding on bright blue moss.

"There they are!" A child on the opposite shore yelled and pointed.

The children ran for the river and jumped in, their heads bobbing in the water.

"Why does it always have to be crazy children chasing after me?" Toby muttered. He pushed his way onto a small area of the bank where the ledge between water and wall was less than a foot wide.

The children reached the opposite bank. They climbed out and rushed towards them.

"We have got to move!" Jurn squeezed in with Toby. "This moss is so slick."

"Just follow the river." Toby reached behind him to grab Jurn's shirt sleeve. "Stay close behind me. Step where I step and I'll try to shine the light for both of us.

The passage cut a sharp right and for a moment the boys were alone. The cavern split into two tunnels. One continued to border the river, and the other slanted upwards.

"I vote for dry ground," said Toby.

"But we don't know where the passage leads. Let's stick to the plan." Jurn slid past Toby.

"Stop, it's too dangerous!" Toby ran after his friend, but the boy moved quickly, and Toby could only train the light on his vanishing figure.

The space between wall and river narrowed again, and soon the boys splashed through ankle-deep water.

Toby caught up with Jurn. "Watch out for drop-offs, The cavern river back home has some nasty ones."

They scampered around another turn. Toby stopped short. "Oh no, the tunnel's almost closed up!" He shone the flashlight across the room.

Much of the ceiling had collapsed, and rocks almost blocked the water flow.

"Maybe these cut off the town's supply." Jurn ran to the pile of rocks. "How do we get out? It would take weeks to move all of this!"

More cries from behind them.

Toby shone his light on the dark liquid's surface. Boulders held the water back to create a deep pool. "If this water was stagnant, algae would be floating on it. Besides, I can hear it flowing on the other side, so there has to be a way through." Toby followed the faint tinkling and stopped. "It's coming from this area."

He shone the light towards the pool. A large log was jammed in a pile of stones, causing an open wedge. The water gushed through in joyous freedom.

"It's big enough for us to fit through." Jurn threw himself into the deep pool and began to swim for the log.

"I hate water." Toby groaned. But there was no other way, so he pulled off his coat, threw it to the side, and plunged into the icy stream after his friend.

Now Jurn was the one to call back words of encouragement. "Come on, Toby, plenty of room here.

You can make it."

Toby's flashlight made crazy patterns in the water as it swung from his teeth.

The shouts of the children died away, and Toby could only hope they thought the boys had taken the dry path.

"The water's almost stopped here, Toby." Jurn's voice echoed back. "Hey, lights!

Faint voices called out, and Toby's heart sank. Had Simper and the children circled around by a different tunnel to catch them?

Toby plunged under a particularly tight spot, and for one nasty instant his tail caught in the rocks. Water choked him while he screamed and thrashed wildly. *I'm going to die. I'm never going to see the grambles or Mia again.* With a mighty, painful jerk, he pulled it free. A moment of desperate paddling, and he pushed to the other side. The water splashed over a steep bank and trickled down to a small stream. He rounded the corner, ready for a fight.

Jurn leaned against a huge iron fence that covered the mouth of the tunnel from floor to ceiling.

The flashlight beam brightened with Mr. Malachi's smile. "Hey, you made it. Wow. Did not notice those ears. And look at your tail. Incredible!"

"Mr. Malachi, what are you doing here?" Toby yelled above the clang of metal. Several elderly men banged on the fence with broken metal pipes and other makeshift tools.

Mr. Malachi wiped his forehead with a rag. "Some of the vibrant ones created a bit of a disturbance. It took me some time to break it up and get people calmed down. Afterwards, I went into the Palace and couldn't find you two, so I figured you must have discovered a way to get down here. And how were you going to push through this big fence?" He peered into the darkness. "I'm sorry, son.

Did you find another tunnel out?"

"No." Jurn gestured behind them. "There's a huge pile of rocks, and the river's barely flowing. I don't think we can go back, and even if we did, Simper's after us."

Toby gave the fence a shake. "It looks pretty stuck."

"I know. We're trying." Mr. Malachi's knuckles whitened around the handle of his crude hammer.

A rumbling sound came from behind the wall. "This place isn't stable!" Toby shouted. "We really need to move out."

Tiny bits of dust and gravel showered down on Jurn's face. "Please hurry." He pushed against the fence.

Toby banged his small body against the bars.

"We won't leave you, Toby," Mr. Malachi wedged a metal rod into a space. "I'll get you out of here."

"No, I will!" Marabella flew into the light of Mr. Malachi's torches. She ran to the fence. "Everyone, move outta the way!" She pulled out the metal saw Jurn had been using to repair the roamer.

"You sneaky thief!" Jurn shrieked. "I wondered where that went! Give it to me!"

"No way!" Marabella's fingers fumbled with the switch, then the blade was moving. She pressed it against the fence. A shower of sparks lit up the cave. One bar, then two… the saw bit into the metal like toast.

The men worked to push the bars out of the way. Stones continued to fall and bounce around them, but no one stopped until Toby and Jurn wiggled through to the other side. They all grabbed torches and the precious tools and ran.

Mr. Malachi led them through a short passage. A cookie-shaped patch of daylight grew bigger, until they all stumbled into the fresh air, blinking in the haze of the city streets.

The pastor counted heads. "Praise Jesus, we are all safe." He grabbed Marabella in one of his giant hugs. "Thanks to you, young lady."

Marabella stiffened and turned red. "Okay, yeah. Whatever." She waited until the big man released his hold and stepped back a few feet.

Jurn gave her a hug of his own. "We'd probably be dead if not for you!"

"Well, I guess it was pretty great." A smile spread across her face. "But I'm keeping this." She held up her saw.

"I can't believe we didn't remember the saw. We could have skipped the whole trip through the palace," Toby said.

"But then we wouldn't know how the Vibrance was made," Jurn reminded him.

"Besides, I had it." Marabella said.

While Toby squeezed the water out of his tail, he told Mr. Malachi about Simper, the children, and the wild chase through the tunnels.

"Don't you worry," Mr. Malachi frowned. "Simper has more important things to deal with right now besides running after you. I just hope the children didn't get hurt."

"The river is choked by rocks, right past the fence where it bends." Toby sat on a broken wall. "The ceiling has been crumbling in, a little at a time. The Palace could fall into the ground at any moment, and your water supply would disappear with it."

Malachi rubbed his chin. "Bad news indeed, and no simple answers." He picked up a bag of tools. "The area with the gate is over there, under those buildings. No one lives in that area, so I think we're safe to get supper and discuss what to do next."

9

HOPE

Emory poked at his peas with his spoon and tried to catch them before they rolled off his plate. He still wasn't very hungry, but he needed to stay strong and keep fighting for Sonda. He would try each day, until every idea had been exhausted. But the mood at dinner had dribbled more worry into his heart. The tiniest bite stuck in his throat and expanded until it was impossible to force down.

The strange cat-boy who called himself a Trilby still talked with the other boy, Jurn. Mr. Malachi stood over them, nodding from time to time. They had come in from the Palace an hour ago, wet and covered in mud. Emory couldn't hear what they were saying, but each face looked serious.

He abandoned his peas and scooted his chair closer to catch their words.

"Everyone in town always boils and filters water before they drink it, and somehow that must remove the effects from the Vibrance," Mr. Malachi said.

"It's a good thing," Jurn replied. "Otherwise, the children would have died, right?"

Mr. Malachi pursed his lips. "We have to do something about the water supply. I'm wondering if the water has been diverted through a tunnel you didn't see, or perhaps it hollowed out a stream farther below. Either way, we will have to go in and explore again."

The cat-boy's ears swayed when he nodded. "You'll have to brace up the ceiling, and it'll be dangerous. Then there's the larger area where the children collected the Vibrance. The ceiling could fall in and kill everyone above and below."

Emory sighed. The dancers in the Palace would never leave. Whether the Palace crumbled or the Vibrance took its toll, they were all lost. And nothing anyone said or did could stop it. He laid his head down on the table, despite a sticky pool of spilled gravy.

A small, gloved hand rested on his shoulder.

"Emory, I'm Toby." Toby's large eyes were green like spring leaves, and fringed with thick, dark lashes. His small nose curved at the tip. Feline ears stuck out on top of his head, pink on the inside, and covered with short, dark fur on the outside.

Emory didn't want to stare, but found it very hard to tear his eyes away from those ears. "How old are you?" He instantly wished he could take the question back. Maybe it wasn't very polite.

But Toby's mouth curved into a smile. "I'm fifteen. Mr. Malachi was telling me about your helicopter, and how you like machines and stuff. Maybe you would like to come live with me, at my house. We have a safe place, and people who will love and care for you, just like Mr. Malachi does."

"Do you have books?" Emory asked.

"Oh yes. Thousands. Tens of thousands!"

Thousands of books! All the things I could learn!

"I want to, so very much. But what about Sonda?"

Toby bowed his head. "She's welcome, but I don't know…"

Mr. Malachi rested his hand on Emory's shoulder. "Son, Toby has been telling me about a dangerous group of people in the area. If they came through this town they might take you away. I never should have let you study so much about machines."

"Don't blame yourself. You didn't know about Leader." Toby turned to Emory. "Leader has running cars and trucks. If he finds out about your skills, he would force you to work for him. With me, you'd be protected."

"But Sonda… I don't want to leave her." Emory's breaths came in ragged gasps and his chest heaved.

Mr. Malachi hugged him close. "I know son, I know. Don't give up hope."

Evening birds roosted in the tree at the entrance to the Palace, cooing and settling into their chosen beds. Emory watched them, wishing he could feel that content, just one more time. But after tonight, when he left Sonda, he would be leaving the tiny chance to have a piece of his family back again. His head throbbed. Could they stop the music, just for one night?

She slunk out of the door and almost walked past him. He reached out. "Sonda." He couldn't bring himself to touch her arm.

"Oh, hey. Simper went off somewhere, and then Mitts made me leave. Did you bring me some mems?" Her eyes held more confusion than ever.

His shoulders sagged. "No, Sonda. I just needed to tell

you something. I'm going to a new home. I'm leaving and you might not see me again."

She sighed, and the darkness of the city street seemed like daylight compared to the darkness hidden inside of her. "All right. Probably a good thing."

"I gotta tell you something else, Sonda. The Palace isn't safe. These guys said it might fall through the ground, at any time." Emory wanted to fall on the ground and throw a tantrum like a little kid. But he stood up straight and looked Sonda in the eye. "You can come with me and find something better. Even if you don't believe in yourself, I believe in you. I don't want to lose you."

Sonda giggled. "Oh Emory, you silly boy! Don't you know I'm already lost?" She stumbled off down the street.

Emory watched her go. The sadness inside of him was no longer the kind a child would have. It was a dull ache, now, but one he must accept. In that moment, he had grown up. "Goodbye, Sonda," he whispered.

Sunday. Until Toby had first ventured from the cavern three years ago, the day had been an ordinary part of the week, where computers told of date and time. No day or night existed, seasons never changed. Now Toby looked forward to Sundays as time to sit before his Father, to worship Him and listen for His voice.

Mr. Malachi stood at an intricately carved pulpit, reading from a worn Bible.

I'm so glad we came. It's wonderful to hear the word of God from another voice, spoken from another heart. Toby nudged Jurn, whose eyes drooped.

A slight tremor shook the ground under his feet. *Did I imagine that?* Toby glanced at the children's faces surrounding him. All eyes were wide and staring, probably wondering the same thing.

Another quake, this time stronger. Olders stood and Mr. Malachi closed the Bible. "Lord, whatever is going on, keep us safe. And give us the strength and courage to help."

Someone pounded on the huge entrance door. Serephina, who sat in the back row, ran to answer it.

Stance stood in the doorway. His clothes and hair were covered in white dust, and blood trickled down his forehead. "The Palace... it's falling." He staggered inside and collapsed.

Miss Jasmine knelt by his side. "Serephina, get the supplies." She looked up at Mr. Malachi. "You'd better see what happened."

Mr. Malachi pointed at a few of the older men. "You all come with me."

Toby grabbed Jurn's shoulder. "We're coming too."

Mr. Malachi nodded and they followed him out the door.

Clouds of dust met them in the street. Dazed adults and children leaned against the church building. Some cradled broken or bleeding limbs, seemingly oblivious to their injuries. They all stared at where the Palace stood.

Used to stand. The walls had buckled forward, and the tree Toby had used for his escape was toppled into the yard. Piles of brick, concrete and broken boards covered the street where the line of waiting family members usually stood.

The roof lay in broken pieces across the ground. *The whole thing must have collapsed through the cavern, just like I thought.* Toby strained to see through the choking white fog.

Mr. Malachi ran past him, waving his hammer. "Come on, we have to try to help."

Toby's mind snapped back into focus. "Be careful." He followed Mr. Malachi. "I don't know how far the cavern reaches and we could be in danger too."

He pulled his shirt up over his nose and began to pick his way over the rubble where the front door used to be. *Where do I even begin?* To find anyone seemed impossible.

A woman came by him, the green fabric of her dress showing through the white dust. "Not many in there," she said. "Simper sent most of us out. He was angry. He said we were all spies. The worker kids, too." She reached down and picked up a chunk of concrete. "Oh, we'll never get it back," she wailed. "The dancing. Our forgetfulness!"

Toby ran over to Mr. Malachi and tugged at his sleeve. "Did you hear that? Simper cleared most of the building. Most of the people probably escaped!"

Mr. Malachi's eyes shone. "Oh, praise the Lord! Such good news!"

"Toby, Mr. Malachi. Over here!" Jurn shouted.

They hurried over. Jurn pointed to a hill in the rubble, where an arm, bloodied and bruised, stuck out of the rubble.

"That's where Simper's office used to be." A lump formed in Toby's throat. He took the other side of a board Jurn held and together they lifted it off.

They uncovered the desk they had seen the day before, battered but still standing. They continued to clear the rubble around the arm until it's owner was freed.

"Mitts." Jurn bent down and listened to his chest. "His heart's still beating. Let's get him to the church." .

Mr. Malachi called to his helpers and they ran over. After fashioning a stretcher from a broken door, they rolled the big man's body on it and took him off.

A small figure stood by the church. Toby went back over to Emory.

Tears flowed down the boy's cheeks, creating white, muddy streaks. "Sonda... where is she?"

"I don't know." Toby put his arm around the boy's shoulders. "A lady said almost everyone got out... but I haven't seen her."

"If she's safe, why doesn't she come find me?" Emory peered up at him. "She always came before."

"I'm sorry." Toby could think of nothing else to say.

After several hours of tending to the wounded, Toby, Jurn, Emory and Mr. Malachi headed out to the roamer. Jurn pulled a device the size and shape of a deck of cards out of his pocket and pressed the shiny surface. The roamer shimmered into view.

"Wow," Mr. Malachi and Emory said together.

"Where did Marabella go to, anyway?" Toby looked around.

"Right here, Cat kid." Marabella stepped from behind a tree. "Way too much huggin' and stuff going on in there." She eyed Mr. Malachi warily.

"You missed all the action." Toby gestured back towards the town, where a dusty haze still hung over the tree line.

"I've had enough to last me for awhile." Marabella pulled out her saw and polished the blade with her grubby shirt sleeve.

"I was worried you went off to join up with Leader," said Jurn.

"Yeah, I thought about it, but I needed a new bandage." Marabella waved her hand, a slight smile tugging at the corner of her lips.

A huge weight slid off Toby's shoulders. The grambles'

location was still safe, for now. "Welcome back. We're going to have an extra passenger with us. Marabella, this is Emory."

"H'ya, Emory."

The boy gave a shy smile. "Hi."

Toby opened the side panel, and Jurn helped the younger boy climb in. Marabella followed.

Mr. Malachi stood to the side, an amazed grin covering his face. "This thing's from outer space, you say?"

"You wouldn't believe the story if I told you." Toby shook the giant man's hand. "We'll be back to check on you, and bring tools. Gramble Horace might have a suggestion for how to fix your water situation."

Mr. Malachi bowed his head. "I wish I could accept, Toby, but if this Leader person comes through, we can't have an influx of supplies we are unable to explain. Please do send your prayers, though, especially for the poor souls from the Palace. And for Simper."

"Do you think they'll ever find him?" Toby looked back towards the town.

"I don't know. We'll try our best, but if he was down in the mem-hoard it's going to take more resources and manpower than we have to recover his body."

"There has got to be more I can do. You have all these people to take care of." Toby wanted to scream in frustration. *Is this really just another dead end?*

"You have done more than you could ever know." Mr. Malachi enveloped him in a bear hug that nearly lifted him off the ground. "Our next step is to see if we can reroute the flow. We'll be busy taking care of the wounded folks for a while, anyways." He released his hold and patted Toby on the head.

Toby could feel Marabella's smirk behind him, but he hugged Mr. Malachi back. "I can't make the decision alone, but I'll be back."

Mr. Malachi held up his hand. "Toby, we've already had this discussion."

Toby stared into the man's impossibly dark eyes. "It's time for me to stop living in fear. I was called to help people. My family is more than who lives in my home. Every person on this planet is my brother or sister, and that includes the souls in this city. We'll figure it out, and then I will return."

Mr. Malachi nodded slowly. "Go with God, Toby."

Jurn and Marabella led Emory up into the roamer and helped him get settled.

Toby climbed aboard and flipped down the viewer. He spun around. "Everyone ready to go home?"

"Wait!" Emory stood up and pointed at the screen.

A very thin, very white girl ran toward the ship. "Emory! Emory!" she called.

"Sonda!" Emory leaned against the roamer's side panel. "Toby, let me out. She's alive!"

Toby opened the door and the boy almost fell out of the ship in his haste to reach his sister.

"Sonda, please don't make me leave you behind."

"Oh Emory, the walls were cracking!" Sonda gasped. "Simper made the music stop, and we all had to leave. I fell asleep in the ally. Serephina found me and told me you where out here."

Emory grabbed her thin hands in his own. "Please come with me. I'm going to a place that's clean and safe and beautiful, with lots of friends." He turned to Toby, who had followed him out. "She can come too, can't she?"

Toby stared back into the roamer. "It'll be a tight squeeze, but we can make room. Of course she can come." Sonda might have a rough time getting over the Vibrance, but he was sure Gramble Edward could help the girl.

Emory pulled her into the ship and showed her his seat. "You can sit here, I'll just stand."

"Okay." Sonda looked around in wonder.

Toby sat back in the pilot's seat. *What have I gotten myself into?* But every time he listened to Father's voice, only good came of his obedience.

He looked back at Emory. "Are we ready now?"

"Yes, Sir!" Emory shouted.

Toby pulled down the viewer screen once more.

Mr. Malachi stood outside, his hands raised high in the air. Tears streamed down his cheeks while he shouted, through the biggest smile Toby had ever seen. "Never give up hope!"

If someone close to you struggles with addiction, if you are dealing with it personally, or if you just want to know more about God, you can call Focus on the Family at 1-800-A-FAMILY to talk to a trained counselor.

If you have any questions about the subjects in this book, please e-mail the author at <u>atmadunes@aol.com</u>.

About the Author

Angela Castillo's first story, written at the age of 8, was a tale about two children who climbed a rainbow with gum stuck to their shoes. Sadly, this story was lost to humanity but several of her short stories, poems and articles have been published in magazines and online. This is her third book about Toby. You can find out more about the "Toby the Trilby" series at www.tobythetrilby.weebly.com, or "like" www.facebook.com/tobythe trilby.

THE AMAZING ADVENTURES

OF TOBY THE TRILBY

The procession moved slowly. The people were dressed in garments constructed from swamp moss. Hair woven in round, basket-like shapes rested on the shoulders of men and women, shades of umber, silver and white advertised varying ages. Beards hung down almost to the men's waists, hairs curling to meld with their outfits. Toby was fascinated, having never seen so much facial hair except on films. The people marched in silence, resolution covering their tanned, strong faces.

A girl stumbled along in the center of the crowd. She wore a pure white dress, in stark contrast to the rest of the group. Golden hair spilled down her back. She could not hold a torch, since her hands were bound together in front of her.

Why was she a prisoner? Toby's heart beat faster; the girl must be in danger. No weapons were visible, but if discovered he'd be overpowered in an instant. Beads of sweat formed on his forehead despite the cool evening. He didn't dare wipe them off. Perhaps if he followed the group he could find a way to help the girl.

He stayed back while keeping the group in sight, thankful again for his light build. A twig cracked under his foot and he froze. Panic welled up in him then dissipated when no one turned.

The group followed a well-worn path. They crossed a rope bridge, the bound girl stumbling as the structure swayed. The people watched her struggle to regain her balance, but no one offered a hand to assist her.

The procession came to a sudden halt. Coils of serpentine brilliance stretched before the leader of the group. Calmly and without a sound, the man found two sticks and gently moved the snake to the bushes on the side of the path. The march continued.

Small, stifled sounds drifted over the people's shuffled footsteps. Was the fair-haired girl crying?

The path widened, then split in two, circling a large swamp. The glossy, black edges seeped past the view of the torchlight. Patches of slime floated on the surface of the water. A dock made of logs and rope jutted out towards the center, with extra sections of rope coiled to the side. Chunks of rock served as a crude staircase to reach the edifice.

The people placed torches on stakes set a few feet apart. The flames made eerie shapes as they flickered in the breeze. The leader approached the girl. When he turned his face, Toby glimpsed an ancient scar that slashed through his cheeks and lips, disappearing under his white beard.

The man grabbed the girl's bound hands and jerked her towards the dock. She screamed and tried to pull away. A younger man yanked her back and slapped her face. The sound echoed through the swamp.

Help her. Toby fought the instinctive cry in his head. He watched, useless hands gripping branches at his sides, while the men forced her up the steps and to the end of the dock. The girl's shoulders slumped and silent tears coursed over the bright red mark on her beautiful face.

The scarred man raised his hands high in the air. His wild eyes glowed in the lights.

"Oh, Natura," his voice warbled.

"Natura," the crowd echoed.

"Most beautiful Goddess," the man continued.

"Giver of good and terrible things.

Milk sours early,

trees bear bitter fruit,

our children are fitful.

We respect your wishes.

Tiend has come.

We give you this child.

Take her into your body

to nourish your soul.

Take her, and we humbly pray for favor."

Images of human sacrifice flashed through Toby's mind: Incas' offerings of life and limb, stone alters of the druids. Escape from the horrific truth was impossible. This girl would die. Even while he gripped the small penknife, his spirit protested the very idea of plunging it into living flesh. Could he hurt someone, even to save another?

The men grabbed the girl's bound wrists and lowered

her into the water. The action seemed absurd. No sharp weapon, no blood shed.

Water lapped at the girl's knees, harmless at first. She struggled. Inch by inch, her body sank into the mud.

"Please don't do this!" she pled. "Why would your goddess want me? I'm just a girl! Please help!"

The oldest man turned and took his torch down from its stake. The rest of the crowd followed his motion in a single, swift abandonment and filed back down the original path.

Toby wondered if their action was ceremonial or if the people were too squeamish to watch the death of the innocent girl. Whatever the reason, the opportunity surpassed all hope. While his heart screamed "forward!" his brain told him to wait. He counted to one hundred, then snapped on his flashlight and crept to the edge of the pit.

Excerpt from THE AMAZING ADVENTURES OF TOBY THE TRILBY By Angela Castillo. Reprinted with author's permission.

Available at www.tobythetrilby.weebly.com and Amazon.com in paperback and Kindle.